Let's Moose!

based on text by Audrey Fraggalosch
Illustrated by Crista Forest

To Helen, with gratitude — A.F.

To The Friends of Algonquin Park — C.F.

Published by Soundprints Division of Trudy Corporation, Norwalk, Connecticut.

Book design: Marcin D. Pilchowski
Editor: Laura Gates Galvin
Editorial assistance: Chelsea Shriver

First Edition 2003
10 9 8 7 6 5 4 3 2 1
Printed in China

Acknowledgments:
      Our thanks to Dr. James Peel, professor of wildlife resources at the University of Idaho, for his curatorial review.

Library of Congress Cataloging-in-Publication Data is on file with the publisher and the Library of Congress.

Let's Explore, MOOSE!

based on text by Audrey Fraggalosch
Illustrated by Crista Forest

AMAZING ANIMAL ADVENTURES

A note to the reader:
Throughout this story you will see words in **bold letters**. There is more information about these words in the glossary. The glossary is in the back of the book.

A hungry moose **wades** in a lake. **Pondweeds** make a yummy snack for Moose!

Moose returns to
her baby. Baby is
happy to see Moose.
Moose is happy to
see Baby.

Moose brings Baby to the lake. A big **crane** chases Baby! Baby runs to Moose.

Moose goes in the water. Baby goes in the water. Moose teaches Baby to swim.

Soon summer will be over. Moose and Baby eat grass and **twigs**. The more Baby eats, the bigger Baby grows!

A bear gets ready for winter. He eats berries. Moose and Baby also get ready for winter. They eat leaves.

Moose and Baby also eat mushrooms. One day Baby will be as big as a **bull**!

Soon it is winter.
There is snow
all around. Now
Moose and Baby
eat **bark**.

It snows and snows.
The snow is very
deep. It is hard for
Moose and Baby to
run in the snow!

Finally it is spring again! Baby is now a young moose! Young Moose is so big he can live on his own.

Young Moose is hungry.
Young Moose wades in
the lake. Pondweeds
make a yummy snack
for Young Moose!

Glossary

Bark: the tough covering of a tree, root or stem.

Bull: a full-grown male moose.

Crane: a tall bird that wades in water.

Pondweeds: plants with green flowers that grow in lakes and ponds.

Twigs: small branches from trees and shrubs.

Wades: walks in water or mud.

Wilderness Facts
About the Moose

Moose are the world's largest deer,
and the male moose, called a bull,
is the mightiest animal with antlers.
Female moose do not grow antlers.
Bulls stand about seven feet tall and
weigh around 1,400 pounds — that's
as much as a small car!

Bulls shed their antlers every winter
and grow a new pair every spring.
At first the antlers are covered in
"velvet," short, soft fuzz that pro-
tects the growing antlers.

The first time a moose cow has a baby it is usually a single calf, but after that she will often have twins. Moose calves stay with their mothers for at least one year.

Moose are found mainly in the boreal forest — the most common type of forest in North America.

Other animals that live in a Canadian boreal forest:

Black bears

Cranes

Deer mice

Gray wolves

Lynx

Porcupines

Red squirrels